Megan Batastini 5-L

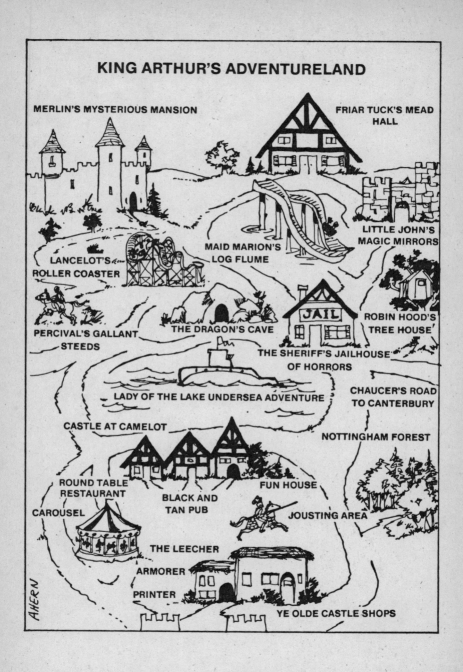

KING ARTHUR'S ADVENTURELAND

MERLIN'S MYSTERIOUS MANSION

FRIAR TUCK'S MEAD HALL

LITTLE JOHN'S MAGIC MIRRORS

MAID MARION'S LOG FLUME

LANCELOT'S ROLLER COASTER

JAIL

PERCIVAL'S GALLANT STEEDS

THE DRAGON'S CAVE

ROBIN HOOD'S TREE HOUSE

THE SHERIFF'S JAILHOUSE OF HORRORS

LADY OF THE LAKE UNDERSEA ADVENTURE

CHAUCER'S ROAD TO CANTERBURY

CASTLE AT CAMELOT

NOTTINGHAM FOREST

ROUND TABLE RESTAURANT

FUN HOUSE

CAROUSEL

BLACK AND TAN PUB

JOUSTING AREA

THE LEECHER

ARMORER

PRINTER

YE OLDE CASTLE SHOPS

AHERN

C.J. Watson Solves the

DRAGON'S BLOOD MYSTERY

by Angelo Resciniti

A Noodle Factory Children's Book Club
Presentation
1980

Dedicated . . .
. . . to Jean Clements for the beginning
. . . to Renaissance, the English band, for the middle
. . . to Paula Muniz for the finish.

I

The Volkswagon mini-bus cruised along Interstate 80 at a steady 55 miles per hour. Its seven passengers sang at the top of their lungs. "We're off to see the wizard, the wonderful Wizard of Oz," they sang over and over again.

"I can't believe it!" exclaimed C. J. Watson during a break in the singing. "Opening day at 'King Arthur's Adventureland.' And we're going to be there. It's unreal!"

"You can thank your Aunt Annie for the honor," said Al Watson, C.J.'s father. "Her company designed all of the special effects used in the amusement park. She wanted to be here in person opening day to make sure they all worked right."

"It's a nice way to get a free vacation for the family," said Annie Watson. She sat in the front passenger seat. Catherine

Watson, C. J.'s mother, drove. "A vice-president has certain privileges. This trip wasn't hard to arrange. I know Nancy and Ronnie like the idea," said Annie Watson.

"I can't wait until we get there!" said Ronnie. He was a year younger than C. J. Nancy was a year older than C. J. They were all cousins.

"The hardest part was getting your Uncle Ron away from his work," said Annie Watson to C. J. Ron and C. J.'s dad were brothers.

"What kind of work do you do, Uncle Ron?" asked C. J. "Mom and Dad won't tell me."

"I work for Uncle Sam," said Ron Watson. Then he quickly launched into another verse of "We're off to see the wizard . . ."

"Boy, C.J.," said Ronnie, "You're lucky to live so close to 'King Arthur's Adventureland.' Florida is so far away from here. If Mom didn't have to come, I don't think we'd ever get here."

"People have been talking about the place for five years now," said C. J. "It's

4

hard to believe it's finally open." Silently, C. J. wondered why Uncle Ron had changed the subject away from his job. He'd have to check that one out later, he thought.

The traffic got thicker as they neared the exit for the amusement park. Billboards along the highway showed drawings of dragons, knights in armor and damsels in distress. There were pictures of King Arthur and Sir Lancelot and Sir Gawain and the other Knights of the Round Table.

"Why were they called 'Knights of the Round Table'?" asked Nancy. "Does anyone know?"

"I know why," said C. J. "Our teachers made us do a lot of research about King Arthur's times. That was the bad part of the amusement park being built nearby. The knights sat at a round table because King Arthur wanted them all to be equal. A round table has no 'head' place. So none of the knights could gain honor by being closer to the head of the table. All 12 of the knights were treated the same way."

"That's really neat!" said Ronnie. "When will we get there, anyway?"

"Look, you can see the castle up ahead!" exclaimed Nancy. "It's just like the castle in *Camelot*, the movie. I'll bet there will be lots of handsome knights all over the place."

C. J.'s mother parked the mini-bus in the parking section named after Sir Bedivere. There were 13 parking lots, one for each knight and one for King Arthur. The seven Watsons rode the tram bus to the front gate of the park.

"Nancy, you watch over these menfolk today," joked her mother. "Keep those two big ones out of trouble. C. J. and Ronnie can take care of themselves."

C. J.'s mother and aunt went into the business entrance of the park. C. J. lined up at the main gate with his dad, his uncle, and his two cousins. Their "special admission" badges got them right into the park. Across a beautiful blue moat stood "The Castle at Camelot." That was the first of the three major areas of "King Arthur's Adventureland."

"We've got until nine tonight," said Al

6

Watson. "So let's begin at the beginning and see it all."

The group was met at the moat by a knight in armor. "Good day, ladies and gentlemen," said the knight through a closed visor. He must have been seven feet tall. "My name is Percival. I would fain show you through the entrance to the castle. Especially since it is a passing fine morning. If you follow me I will gain safe conduct through the gate for all of us."

Sir Percival turned slowly and clanked along the bridge that crossed the moat. His armor shined brightly in the morning sun. C. J. noticed that Sir Percival wore a real broadsword and a wire mesh basket for carrying supplies. C. J. could see a canteen, a bag of raisins, and some green papers through the mesh.

"Hey, smartypants," said Nancy to C.J. "If you're so smart about King Arthur, what the heck do the words 'fain' and 'passing' mean?"

"Easy," answered C. J. " 'Fain' means gladly and 'passing' means exceptionally. Sir Percival said he would gladly show us around on this exceptionally beautiful day."

Sir Percival stopped walking. He turned toward the group. "There is a man of knowledge among you," said the knight. "Young man, come forth. I offer you a gift from King Arthur himself." C.J. stepped up. The knight reached into his mesh basket and pulled out the top one of the green bills. He handed it to C.J. "This certificate will be accepted for a free ride on 'Lancelot's Roller Coaster'," said Sir Percival. "And now, let us continue our perilous journey."

C. J. examined the certificate closely. It was beautifully printed. There was a drawing of King Arthur in the middle. The number "1" was printed in every corner. King Arthur's signature looked just like the real thing. C.J. dropped the coupon into his wallet. It fit perfectly.

The gate to the castle lifted straight up following Sir Percival's shout to the gatekeeper. The knight saluted the group of visitors. He turned and clanked to the other end of the bridge to meet the next group.

C. J. and his group entered the courtyard of the castle. It was an incredible sight. He felt like they had time-traveled to another age. The castle looked just like the pictures in the books C. J. had read.

There were huge tents in every corner of the courtyard. Letters burned into wood named each one. There was "The Round Table Restaurant," "The Black and Tan Pub," "Lady Guinevere's Fun House," "The Carousel," and many more. Colorful streamers fluttered in the breeze. Musicians strolled through the crowd, playing lutes and recorders. The aromas of spicy meats and pastries filled the air.

"Ladies and gentlemen!" shouted a high-pitched voice. C.J. saw that it came from a dwarf dressed in the costume of a court jester. The area fell silent. "I am Mickey Dunn, scop at the court of King Arthur. A scop is a roving minstrel, a bearer of news. And this I announce to you. The first jousting tournament of the day begins in five minutes in the gaming area behind me."

The crowd moved as one to the corner of the courtyard. Knights in full armor

9

were lifted into the air by small cranes with strong ropes. The knights were dropped gently onto the backs of huge horses. One horse was black, the other white. They were covered with ribbons and multi-colored cloths. The knights took up their lances. The horses pranced to opposite ends of a long rope. Each knight wore a scarf around the handle of his lance. They each battled for the honor of a lady.

~ Mickey Dunn, the scop, called for the joust to begin. The crowd held its breath. The horses picked up speed. The knights lowered their lances. The battlers came closer and closer together. They made a pass at each other. Both lances missed the target. The crowd let out a sigh of relief. Then the courtyard filled with applause as the knights saluted each other.

"Boy, that was exciting!" said Nancy. "This place is really great."

"I'm ready for 'The Black and Tan Pub' after that," said C.J.'s father. "The English have always known how to make a good beer."

"I'm afraid you'll be disappointed then," said Uncle Ron. "The only thing that resembles black and tan in there is a root beer float." They all laughed at that.

They all rode the carousel and had a chuckle in "Guinevere's Fun House." They ate tasty beef and mushroom pies in "The Round Table Restaurant." They even had a round of root beer floats in "The Black and Tan Pub."

"The only part of the castle we haven't seen has 'Ye olde Castle Shops' in it," said C. J. "How about if we go there before we leave for 'Nottingham Forest'?"

And so they went over to the row of tents called "Ye Olde Castle Shops." One booth was named "The Leecher." An old woman in loose robes held out a jar of leeches. "Boys and girls," she croaked. "Do you feel poorly this morning? My leeches will balance out your humors. A little blood-letting is good for the body." The old lady cackled when Ronnie backed out of the tent, bumping into his father.

Then they visited Big John Curtis, a giant man who stood beneath a sign that said "Armorer." Big John stood over a

11

suit of armor. He had a welding torch in his giant hand. He welded a shoulder onto the nearly-completed suit of armor.

Finally they entered the booth of "The King's Printer." Sawdust covered the floor. Ancient-looking hand-cranked printing presses turned slowly. On one press C. J. could see page after page of free ride certificates, just like the one in his wallet. An old man turned the crank that ran the press. He turned when C. J. and his family entered the tent. The man had a nameplate on his deerskin jacket. It said, "Manny Ninger, Printer of Royal Documents."

In the back of the printing tent a number of old-looking barrels were piled up. In stencil lettering on each was printed, "Dragon's Blood." Nearby were stacks of wood crates. In stencil lettering on each of the crates was printed, "Crane and Co., Dalton, Mass."

C. J. wanted to ask the man about the certificates. He wanted to know the process for making them so beautiful.

"Mr. Ninger. . ." began C.J. He was interrupted by a loud commotion outside
12

the tent. They all ran outside to take a look.

Big John Curtis, the armorer, stood near the exit of "The Black and Tan Pub." He had a huge hand wrapped around the arm of a neatly-dressed man. The man flailed his arms. He was shouting, loudly, "Get your paws off me, you big ape! How dare you put your mitts on Tony Palermo! I'll sue! I swear I'll sue!"

A large crowd gathered around the scene. Sir Percival, Manny Ninger, Mickey Dunn, other park workers and lots of visitors stood and watched. A tall man dressed just like Mickey Dunn ran over. He took Tony Palermo's other arm. With Big John he hustled the man through a door in the wall of the castle.

"Don't worry, folks," said Sir Percival. "Please go on and enjoy. These things happen, you know. Let the festivities continue."

C. J. saw Sir Percival reach into the mesh basket for the free ride tickets. Mickey Dunn ran over and put his hand into the basket. He carefully lifted coupons from the top of the stack and put

13

them into Percival's hand. Sir Percival tossed the coupons into the air. People scrambled for the free ride tickets. The arrest was forgotten.

"Thank you, little one," said Percival to Mickey Dunn. "The basket is indeed difficult to reach in my armor."

Dunn ran off without a word. He patted Manny Ninger on the shoulder. Then he announced the next jousting tournament.

C.J. noticed that Uncle Ron had disappeared during the commotion. He asked his father where Uncle Ron had gone.

"I don't know," said C. J.'s dad. "But I think it had something to do with the arrest."

Seconds later Uncle Ron emerged from a door in the wall of the castle. He walked with Big John Curtis and a man dressed in a jester costume. Big John went back to his booth. But the jester came along with Uncle Ron.

"Folks, I'd like you to meet Beowulf," said Uncle Ron. "Actually, he's Stephen

Greene, head of security here, and an old buddy of mine." They said hello all the way around. "Steve tells me that Palermo was passing a counterfeit $20 bill in the pub. Palermo is only the most famous faker in the country today."

"We had him dead to rights," said Beowulf/Greene. "He insisted that this time he was innocent, though. He said he got the twenty in change here at the park. He's screaming and yelling for his lawyer. I guess they don't call him 'The Wizard' for nothing. He's sure trying to beat this rap."

"That's funny," laughed Nancy. "We sang 'We're off to see the wizard' all the way here this morning. And what do you know. We get to see 'The Wizard' in person."

They all laughed.

"How about if we go to 'Nottingham Forest'," suggested Uncle Ron. Now, more than ever, C. J. wondered what his uncle did for a living. He also wondered if "The Wizard" was really guilty of passing bad money.

II

The Watsons walked along the shaded path that led to "Nottingham Forest." That was the second section of "King Arthur's Adventureland." All of the attractions in "Nottingham Forest" involved Robin Hood and his band of Merry Men. It also involved their famous enemy, the Sheriff of Nottingham. The path on which they walked was called "Chaucer's Road to Canterbury." It was named after the famous English piece of writing by Geoffrey Chaucer. In *The Canterbury Tales* a group of people told stories during a long journey.

"Do you know very much about counterfeiting?" C. J. asked his Uncle Ron.

"You could say it's one of my hobbies," said Ron Watson. "What would you like to know?"

"What makes Tony Palermo such a famous counterfeiter?"

16

"Palermo actually worked for the Treasury Department at one time," said Uncle Ron. "He was an engraver. He made the plates used to print the bills. His specialty was with twenty dollar bills. He was the best platemaker in the whole department."

"One day Palermo was caught trying to leave the building with a set of plates. He said he was just going to do some extra work at home that evening. His bosses didn't believe him, even though he had a clean record. So they fired him," finished Uncle Ron.

"I can guess the rest," said C. J. "Palermo made his own plates and printed his own bills. How did he get caught?"

"The paper was wrong," said Uncle Ron. "The government uses a special rag paper with colored fibers mixed into it. Only one company makes it and they're not allowed to sell it to anyone but the government. In fact, every sheet of paper is counted about a dozen times. The blank sheets are counted. And the paper is counted every step of the way until the paper money is sent into circulation."

"If he got caught, why is he called 'The

Wizard"?" asked C. J.

"Well, he got about half a million dollars into circulation before he was caught," said Uncle Ron. "And when he got out of jail he did it all over again. He's been busted about half a dozen times, not including today."

"Does he always pass twenties?"

"He did at first. But in recent years he's been specializing in hundreds. It surprised me today when he got caught with an 'Andrew Jackson'," added Uncle Ron.

"Was it the paper that got him caught today?" asked C. J.

"You sure have a lot of questions," chuckled his uncle. "No, it wasn't the paper. And that's the scary part. In the 100 years that this company has been making our paper, not one sheet has been stolen. But that looked like genuine paper that Palermo passed today. The color was wrong this time. Plus it didn't pass the water test. Beowulf Greene let the twenty soak in water. It separated into two sheets of paper, like a sandwich. American dollars are printed on a single sheet of paper."

18

"But Mr. Greene was sure Palermo passed the bill on purpose?" C. J. half-asked, half-stated. "I thought criminals didn't usually change their M.O., their method of operation."

"A counterfeiter is a counterfeiter," said Uncle Ron. "And anyway, this does resemble another famous case. In 1897 a couple of guys used a new photo process to print hundreds the same way. The water test caught them, too. The bills felt thick to the touch. And the color wasn't quite right. The Treasury Department had to call back a whole series of bills —$26 million—because of the fakes. That way shopkeepers could check serial numbers for fake bills. That's the only time that ever happened."

"If you guys don't mind," interrupted Nancy. "We've been standing here for ten minutes. Personally, I'd like to go into 'Nottingham Forest'."

C. J. turned red with embarrasment. "I'm sorry," he said. "I'm just curious about counterfeits. That's a real interesting hobby, Uncle Ron. Can you tell me more about counterfeits later?"

"Sure, C. J. But for now, let's enjoy the amusement park."

Nancy, Ronnie, and C. J. climbed through "Robin Hood's Treehouse." They all went on a tour through "The Sheriff's Jailhouse of Horrors." Perfectly-carved wax figures of famous criminals seemed to come to life in the dark. They told all about their dastardly crimes. Jack the Ripper, Al Capone, Billy the Kid, Bluebeard, Mata Hari, Mr. Hyde, John Dillinger, Genghis Khan, and many other bad guys told their horrible stories.

"This place gives me the creeps," said Nancy.

"Any famous counterfeiters in here?" asked C. J. with a laugh.

"A lot of people wouldn't find that funny," said Uncle Ron, without a laugh. He looked all around. Nobody had been listening. "I imagine the security people here are very uptight after the arrest of Palermo."

"I was just kidding," said C. J. On the way out he saw more barrels with the "Dragon's Blood" label. The barrels were stacked near the wax-working equipment.

20

"Dad, what's 'Dragon's Blood' used for?" asked C. J. "Does that have anything to do with Aunt Annie's work here?"

"As a matter of fact it does," said C.J.'s dad. "That stuff is made by her company. It's a chemical that has many uses. The wax-workers use it while making their figures. A strong acid cuts into the wax. 'Dragon's Blood' is used to stop the engraving action of the wax. It's also used in varnishes and such. I use it in my woodshop to help put finishes on the wood."

"Maid Marian's Log Flume" was next up in their tour of "Nottingham Forest." The Watsons had to wait in line for this ride. C. J. took the opportunity to ask more questions of his Uncle Ron. C. J. was quite curious about counterfeiting by now.

"Uncle Ron, who was the best conterfeiter ever?" asked C.J.

"I don't believe you, C.J.," said Nancy, rolling her eyes. "Why can't we just have some fun today. You're always on the trail of some mystery. You're the most curious 11-year-old I've ever met."

"It's all right, Nancy," said her father. "I don't mind C.J.'s questions."

"So there," said C.J.

"So you want to know about the best ever," repeated Uncle Ron. "I guess that would have been a fellow who lived in New Jersey in the late 1890's. His name was Emmanuel something-or-other. He was a great artist. He bought paper that was almost exactly like the real thing. It was even made by the same Massachusetts company. He simply hand-drew the bills on rag paper. His ink was right. His drawings were right. Only the paper wasn't exactly right. The paper lacked the colored fibers. He passed hundreds of bad dollars before he was caught."

"What happened to him?" asked a wide-eyed Ronnie.

"He went to jail," said his father. "And he disappeared after his release. No one ever heard from him or his family after that. The government lost track of him completely."

They neared the front of the line at "Maid Marian's Log Flume." Young workers worked nearby on the hulls of logs that had been pulled out of the water. The workers swabbed the bottoms with a thick, gooey chemical. The chemical came from barrels marked "Dragon's Blood."

"There sure is a lot of that stuff around this place," said C.J. "Aunt Annie's company must make a lot of it."

"It's the only company that makes it anymore," said Uncle Ron. "And they sell more of it to 'King Arthur's Adventureland' than any other buyer."

They all got slightly soaked riding the log flume.

"I think a round of hot chocolate would go great right now," suggested Uncle Ron. "Let's go over to 'Friar Tuck's Mead Hall.' My treat."

Nancy, Ronnie, and C.J. ran on ahead. Ronnie ran smack into Mickey Dunn, the midget scop, at the doorway of "Friar Tuck's." They fell down together in a tangled heap of arms and legs. A pile of free ride tickets scattered all over the ground. C.J. bent over to pick them up for the minstrel.

"Get away from here, you kid!" screeched Mickey Dunn. "Keep your hands off those tickets. And get out of here!"

"I was just trying to help," said C.J., backing away from the dwarf. "I wasn't going to take any."

Mickey Dunn scrambled to pick up the handbills. He stuffed them rapidly into his pockets. Grabbing the last handful, he ran off.

"Are you all right?" asked C.J.'s father. He and his brother arrived at the end of the scene. "What happened?"

"That little man knocked me over!" cried Ronnie through some tears. "I ripped my jeans."

"He wasn't very nice," said Nancy. "I thought people who worked in these places were supposed to be real nice."

"He was hiding something," said C.J. "We scared him."

"There you go after a mystery again," said Nancy. "Personally, I'd rather have that hot chocolate. Come on, Ronnie. Dry your tears. We're going to have a good time."

24

Ten hot chocolates and twenty oat-meal cookies later, the Watsons were relaxed. Even Ronnie was smiling again. He dabbed at his scraped knee with a napkin. The bleeding had stopped. The scrape wasn't much to worry about.

"I'll go ahead and pay for this," said Uncle Ron. He picked up the bill and walked over to the cashier. He took out his wallet. He took out a bill and handed it to the cashier. "I'm sorry, but I haven't anything smaller." C.J. saw that it was a fifty, with Ulysses S. Grant's picture on it.

The cashier made change. Uncle Ron looked at the two twenties, then began to slide them into his wallet. He looked at them once again.

"Al, could you come over here," he called quietly to C.J.'s father. "C.J., keep Nancy and Ronnie at the table."

C.J. saw his father huddle with Uncle Ron. They talked very quietly, looking over the twenties. C.J. couldn't hear what they were saying. But he did spot the cashier. The man wore a long brown robe, just like Friar Tuck. The man was

25

edging out of the restaurant. C.J. saw him slide out a side door. C.J. saw that his father and uncle hadn't noticed. So he, too, slid out the door.

In the sunlight, C.J. saw the cashier pull the robe over his head and drop it into a trash can. The man wore jeans and a blue work shirt. The man looked around to see if he had been followed out. He didn't notice C.J. standing near the doorway. The man started walking, quickly, toward "Little John's Magic Mirrors." C.J. followed.

The man waved to the ticket-taker and walked right into the building. C.J. waited a few seconds before showing his ticket and entering the house of mirrors.

In the first room were mirrors that distorted a person's image. One mirror made C.J. small. The next made him tall. Another mirror made him skinny. The next made him so very fat. Another mirror gave him a big head. Another one gave him gigantic feet. C.J. giggled as he passed the mirrors. He knew the man would not stop in this room.

C.J. entered the second room. This

one was a maze with mirrors on all the walls. C.J. saw himself reflected in front of him, in back of him, and on both sides of him. The maze slowed him down in his chase. But he knew better than to go too fast. One wrong turn and he could go crashing through a glass wall. And that would hurt!

At the end of the maze C.J. walked into a room with mirrors on the floor and the ceiling. The walls were black and cushioned. The floor started tilting this way and that. C.J. laughed as he spilled over and lay there staring into his own face. He got up just in time to be rolled into a corner of the room. The wall gave way. He spun into another room. The door slammed shut behind him.

C.J. looked around. But he couldn't see anything. The room was in complete darkness. A loudspeaker crackled to life. A ghastly laugh echoed in the room. C.J. heard soft breathing from nearby. He wasn't alone in the room. He felt the hair on the back of his neck stir. More laughs rumbled from the speakers.

Suddenly, the lights blazed on. C.J.

shielded his eyes. He was in a huge room. The walls, floor, and ceiling were all mirrored. Everywhere he looked he saw himself. His head began to spin. He couldn't feel his feet on the ground. Then he saw another reflection in the mirrors. The cashier! The man was pushing against the mirrors somewhere in the room. He was trying madly to get out of the place.

C.J. plopped to the floor. He landed on the seat of his pants. He heard another plop. Then the lighting changed. He could see **through** the mirrors now. Ghouls and monsters and ugly creatures of the night seemed to walk right through the walls. C.J. hugged his knees and tried to stop shaking. He'd have to talk to Aunt Annie about the special effects in this place. They sure were special.

Finally the monsters faded. Soft lights came on in the room. The loudspeaker buzzed to life again. "Thank you for visiting the house of mirrors," said a soft voice. "We hope you found many fine reflections inside. Please exit through the door on your right."

C.J. quickly looked to the right. A
28

glassed door swung open. C.J.'s eyes jumped around the room. He was alone! The cashier had somehow escaped!

C.J. exited "Little John's Magic Mirrors" and walked back to the restaurant. He found his father and uncle outside. They were talking with Mr. Greene.

"Where'd you run off to?" asked C.J's father.

"I followed the cashier when he ran away from the restaurant. He shook me in the house of mirrors."

"That's quite some detective you have for a son, Al," joked Uncle Ron. "C.J., can you describe the man to Mr. Greene."

C.J. gave Mr. Greene a complete description of the man. Then he noticed that Mr. Greene was wearing a suit and tie. He had taken off the Beowulf disguise.

"Are you off duty?" asked C.J.

"As a matter of fact, I'm on duty now," said Mr. Greene. "You probably guessed that the cashier passed a phoney twenty to your uncle. That's the fifth bogus bill to surface today. It looks like a big counterfeiting problem. So I'm on it full-time."

"I thought you were the security chief

here at the park," said C.J.

Mr. Greene laughed. "You helped me out, C.J., so I'm going to let you in on a little secret." He fished his wallet out of a pocket in his suit coat. C.J. saw a shoulder holster beneath the jacket. Mr. Greene flashed open his wallet. C.J. could see a badge. On it was engraved, "Department of the Treasury, United States Government" and "Special Agent."

"You're with the Secret Service!" exclaimed C.J. "You're a real, live T-Man!"

"For sure, young man," said Mr. Greene. "And now for another surprise— so is your Uncle Ron."

III

"It's no wonder you wouldn't tell any-one what you did for a living," said C.J. to his Uncle Ron. The pair lagged behind the rest of the group. They walked along a gravel path to "The Knights of the Round Table" section of the amusement park. "I never realized we had a secret agent in the family!"

"Well, I'm no James Bond, that's for sure," chuckled Ron Watson. "But I do enjoy a 'top secret' clearance with Uncle Sam. And some of my cases do get pretty dangerous, too, just like old 007."

"But really, Uncle Ron," said C.J. "Why did Mr. Greene tell me that he and you were with the Secret Service? That's not a real good way to keep a secret, telling an 11-year-old like me."

"C.J.'s uncle had a very serious expres-sion on his face. "We had to tell you, C.J., for your own protection. The counterfeiters know that you've been chasing after one of their runners. They'll be afraid that you saw something. They'll be afraid that we'll find out."

"They might try to stop you from talking, nephew," added Uncle Ron. "Not even your father knows this yet. But I'm afraid that you're in some danger. I'm going to stay real close to you during the rest of our visit here."

C.J. felt a chill ride up and down his backbone. He didn't know if he was scared or excited. Or both. C.J. decided he'd stay close to Uncle Ron for the rest of the day.

"How long have you been with the Treasury Department?" C.J. asked.

"Oh, about 12 years," said his uncle. "I was hired right after my tour of duty in Vietnam with the Marines. I received a lot of special training that helped me qualify."

"Has the Secret Service been around for a long time?" asked C. J.

"More questions, huh?" laughed Uncle Ron. "I guess it's better to ask questions than to be worried. Well, the Secret Service began on July 5, 1865. Abraham Lincoln got the idea rolling. But Andrew Johnson was President when it officially began.

"You see, C.J., until 1863 there was no single type of paper money used everywhere in America," Ron Watson continued. "Many, many banks issued paper money. And during the Civil War banks in the South issued Confederate money. It was a mess. But it was heaven for counterfeiters. Who could tell a fake from the real thing? At one time nearly one-third of the paper money in circulation was fake. The Secret Service took care of that problem."

"But people still try to pass fake money," said C.J. "Do many people get away with it?"

"Nope, and I'm proud of it. Less than one percent of the bogus cash gets onto the streets. We catch the rest.

"But I'll let you in on a little secret," said Uncle Ron to C.J. "The problem at this amusement park is one of the biggest we've ever faced. We've picked up maybe half a dozen bad bills. There's probably hundreds of dollars of bad stuff floating around here. If we don't put a lid on this case soon, there could be a very big problem."

"What about Tony Palermo? Doesn't his arrest wrap the thing up?" C.J. felt like he was part of the case now.

"Maybe it does," said Uncle Ron. "But maybe it doesn't. We know he was caught passing a bad bill. We know he has a record. But he only had the one bad bill. There is a lot more than one bad bill in this place. So we're still looking."

C.J. and his uncle joined the rest of the family at the entrance to "Lady of the Lake Undersea Adventure."

"I just love this section of the park," said Nancy with a sigh. "The knights are so romantic. There is magic and there are monsters. What a grand time that would have been to live in!"

They all climbed into the wood-covered submarine to take the undersea ride. They sat on wooden benches facing a row of thick glass portholes. Engines came to life with a soft hum. The boat pulled out into the deep blue lagoon.

Beautiful tropical fishes swam past the portholes. The first display to come into sight was a model of Stonehenge. Stonehenge was built in England before the time of King Arthur, C.J. explained to his family members. The circle of stone slabs was rediscovered in modern times. In 1979 scientists pretty well proved that Stonehenge was built so ancient men could time the seasons and the stars. "That discovery showed us that there was a lot of knowledge in the old days," finished C.J.

The last display was very simple. An arm extended from the silt on the lagoon's bottom. And from the arm flashed a beautiful, shining sword.

"Excalibur!" exclaimed C.J. "That's King Arthur's sword, Excalibur. That's how the story of the 'Lady of the Lake' began. Legend has it that King Arthur saw the sword being held just above the surface of the lake. The lady gave him the sword. Excalibur protected King Arthur from injury."

"But I thought King Arthur pulled Excalibur out of a block of stone," interrupted cousin Ronnie.

"That's another version of the legend," said C.J. "We'll be trying it out later in this part of the park."

They saw Mr. Greene of the Secret Service outside of the ride. He called Uncle Ron over. They spoke in whispers for several minutes. Uncle Ron returned.

"I have to go for a little while," said C.J.'s uncle. "I'll meet you at 'Gawain's Public Eating House' in about an hour for dinner. Enjoy the rides. And stay out of trouble." Uncle Ron winked at C.J., but he wasn't smiling. C.J. knew there was big trouble in the park.

C.J. felt frustrated. He wanted to do something to help his uncle and Mr. Greene. Maybe he really had seen something that could help, he thought.

"Lancelot's Roller Coaster" was next. The track curled up and around huge trees and through starry-skied domes. The roller coaster was the best ever for C.J. But he couldn't really enjoy it. What if they fixed it so the car jumped the track? What if a sniper shot at him? C.J. felt like an easy target sitting in the front

36

seat of the car, right behind the unicorn's single-horned head.

C.J., Nancy, Ronnie, and C.J.'s dad lined up to ride "Percival's Gallant Steeds." The brightly-colored ponies trotted alone along a curving track, ducking in between trees and through small, colorful tents. C.J. wondered if he should chance it. But those ponies were so beautiful in the late afternoon sun. He had to take a ride. What could happen on the back of a pony?

C.J.'s pony had a straw-colored mane and dark brown leather reins. A thin saddle melted into a beautiful blanket covered with yellow and brown squares. C.J. straightened his back and rode proudly. He felt on top of the world. What danger? What counterfeiters? What problems?

The pony snorted. C.J. heard a rustling in the bushes near the track. The pony coughed. Then it pawed the ground nervously. C.J. looked around. He didn't see anything. He heard more movement in the bushes. He dug his heels gently into the side of the pony.

Suddenly the pony reared into the air. Its front legs pawed the blue sky. C.J. dug his face into the sandy brown mane. He heard a rush of air past his head. He looked up in time to see a huge form move off in the bushes to his left. And to the right, buried deeply into a tree trunk, was an arrow. The feathers still shook violently. The arrow had just hit. And C.J. had been the target.

The pony took off running. C.J., who had let go of the reins, toppled over backwards. He landed in the sawdust, face first. He got up slowly. As he brushed himself off, he looked through wide eyes at the arrow in the tree. The quivering of the arrow stopped. But the shaking had just begun inside of him.

C.J.'s father arrived first. Right behind him was Mickey Dunn, the dwarf scop.

"Are you all right, son?" asked C.J.'s dad.

"I think so."

"What happened, lad, did the horse throw you?" asked Mickey Dunn in his high-pitched voice.

"Yes. Sort of. I think so," said C.J.

"Dad, could you pull that arrow out of the tree."

"Now, sonny boy, we can't have you taking arrows out of the park," said the scop. "They're made right here and are very, very expensive."

"Dad, you could say that the arrow is what distracted the pony," said C.J. He was regaining control now. He had to get a look at the arrow. "The arrow should probably be removed to keep that from happening again. I don't want to keep it. But I would like to look at it."

"Mr. Dunn?" asked C.J.'s father.

"It makes goodly sense to me," said the midget minstrel. "But I deny you the right to take it out of the pony ring."

Mr. Watson reached up and yanked at the arrow. The shaft didn't budge. He yanked again. This time it came free. He handed the arrow to C.J.

C.J. examined the arrow. The wood was newly-cut. The shaft had been treated, but not varnished. C.J. wondered if "dragon's blood" had been used for the finish. The feathers were new and the glue was fresh. The arrowhead was beautifully crafted. The metal was bright and shiny. The shape was perfect. The arrow would have flown straight and true. Had the horse not reared up. . . .

C.J. handed the arrow over to Mickey Dunn. The midget ran off through the crowd that had gathered. Sir Percival made another one of his appearances. He gave out more free ride coupons. The knight gave C.J. a healthy handful.

"I apologize for the steeds," said the knight. "If you would like a free ride on the same pony, I would gladly arrange it."

"Uh," paused C.J. "Maybe later. I feel like moving on for right now."

"So be it!" said Percival. He clanked off in the opposite direction. He pulled more tickets from his mesh basket. A group of children followed closely on his shiny metal heels.

"C.J., did that arrow really have something to do with your fall?" asked Mr. Watson of his son.

"Yes, it did." C.J. was still shaking. He bit his lip to keep the tears from starting. He didn't want to betray what Uncle Ron had told him. But this was his father. He didn't know what to do. So he said, again, "Yes, it did." Then he bit down a little harder.

"Well, we have a little while yet before we meet Ron," said C.J.'s dad. "Let's hit 'Excalibur' and 'Merlin's Mysterious Mansion' before we meet before dinner. Then we can visit 'The Dragon's Cave' after dinner."

"Excalibur" was based on the other legend of King Arthur's famous sword. A huge broadsword was buried nearly to the hilt in a block of granite rock. The object of the game was simple. A computer asked the contestant a series of trivia questions. Every time the player got one right the sword pulled a few inches out of the rock. Ten correct answers and the sword dangled freely from an invisible wire. And the winning player received a small replica of "Excalibur" in a shiny scabbard.

C.J., Nancy, Ronnie, and C.J.'s dad watched as player after player failed to get the sword out of the stone. Every time the sword edged away a few inches people in the crowd clapped. Fifteen straight players failed to get the needed ten correct answers.

"You're pretty smart, C.J.," said Ronnie. "Why don't you try it."

"Go ahead, C.J.," said Nancy. "We're with you all the way."

"I'll try it," said C.J. But, he thought, I'm not going to stand under the sword as it swings around. With my luck, he shuddered, it would probably cut my head off.

C.J handed the gatekeeper one of the free ride tickets from the wad he now carried in his wallet. People in the crowd cheered as he stood before the brightly-lit computer panel. C.J. punched in for the first question.

"Name the science officer on the U.S.S. Enterprise."

"Mr. Spock," answered C.J. The sword pulled out a few inches.

"Name the pilot of the 'Millennium Falcon'."

"Han Solo" He had seen *Star Wars* four times. The sword edged out further. The cheers grew louder.

The questions increased in difficulty.

C.J. kept answering correctly. He had just finished number nine. Only the tip of the sword was still buried in stone. A huge crowd had gathered around to watch C.J. in action.

"Whose picture is on a $50 bill?" A buzz went through the crowd. People dug for their wallets.

"Ulysses S. Grant!" shouted C.J. For a moment, nothing happened. Then the sword jumped out of the stone. The huge blade swung on its invisible wire. The applause of the crowd turned to a stunned silence. The sword headed straight for C.J.!

Without thinking, C.J. jumped down and to the right. He hit the ground hard. The blade smashed into the computer console. A blinding light flashed. C.J. heard the crackle of electricity above his head. Flames leapt from the shattered control panel. The sword hung with its point just inches above C.J.'s head. He saw the flames licking against the thin wire holding the sword aloft. The wire seemed to be melting. . . .

"Run, son, run!" The voice belonged

to his father. "Run, C.J.!"

The shouts broke the spell. C.J. rolled over and over and over until he spilled from the concrete to the softer ground. He heard fire extinguishers. He felt warm hands on his shoulders. He recognized them as his father's. They felt wonderful.

"I'm fine, Dad. Really I am." C.J. felt the shakes coming on again. Some day at the amusement park! C.J. felt cold all over. He saw the blackened control panel. The flames were out. Excalibur lay on the ground, its point shattered. He had been looking up at that point just seconds earlier. Bad luck? Murder attempt?

This time C.J.'s lip-biting didn't work. He felt his father's arm warm around his shoulder as they walked. He saw the ticket-taker come over. The man handed C.J. his prize, a miniature Excalibur in a scabbard. C.J. slid the prize into his rear pocket. He didn't think about winning. He didn't think about counterfeits. He was glad to be with his father right then.

"Feel like eating?" asked Mr. Watson of his son. "We can eat now and then see the haunted house and the cave after dinner. How does that sound?"

Suddenly, C.J. was very hungry. He wanted some food. And then he wanted to get to the bottom of this mystery. He had been shot at with an arrow and attacked with a sword. He had had quite enough!

"Let's eat!" said C.J. Watson, smiling again.

IV

C.J. told his father the whole story along the way to "Gawain's Public Eating House." He made sure Nancy and Ronnie didn't hear.

Uncle Ron was waiting outside the restaurant. He glanced at his watch as they walked up.

"You're a little late," he said. "Anything happen?"

C.J. laughed. "Not much happened," he said. "Someone shot an arrow at me. And then someone tried to chop my head off with a seven-foot sword. That's all that happened."

"Accidents?" asked Uncle Ron, very seriously.

"The sword might have been an accident," said C.J. "But I don't think the arrow was accidental at all."

The five Watsons sat around plates of barbecued ribs. A sizzling tray of fried potatoes and steaming bowls of baked beans topped off the feast.

"Sir Gawain was one of the most famous of King Arthur's knights," said C.J. through a mouthful of beans. He had done plenty of research on the knights. He wanted to share all that work with people other than his teacher at school. "He was dining with King Arthur one night when a stranger dropped in for a visit. The newcomer was the Green Knight. He was dressed all in green. He issued a challenge to all the knights at the banquet. He said he wanted a knight to use an axe to chop off his head."

"What a strange challenge," said Nancy. "Didn't everyone think he was crazy?"

"Many of them thought so," continued C.J. "But the Green Knight made it a point of knightly honor. He insisted that someone had to chop his head off."

"Who ended up doing it?" asked Nancy.

"Sir Gawain did it," said C.J. "But first he accepted the terms of the challenge. The terms were simple. Whoever agreed to chop off the Green Knight's head

48

would have to return the favor a year later."

"That doesn't make sense," said Ronnie. He had stopped eating to listen to the tale. If the Green Knight's head was cut off, how could he cut off Gawain's head a year later?"

"That's what all of the knights figured, too." said C.J. "So Gawain took his axe and lopped off the Green Knight's head. Blood spurted all over the place. . . ."

"This is terrible dinner conversation!" interrupted C.J.'s father. "Can't this wait until later?"

"What happened, C.J.? Tell me, please," begged Ronnie.

"Well, the Green Knight stood up and picked up his head," said C.J. He thought back to the sword that had just missed **his** head. He shivered. "He held the head by the hair. And he talked to all of the knights. He said he expected Sir Gawain to find him in a year to repay the debt."

"Did he look for him?" asked Nancy.

"Of course," said C.J. "After all, Sir Gawain was thought to be the most honorable of all the knights. He found the Green Knight. He passed several tests to his honor. The Green Knight refused to chop off Gawain's head. They shook hands and Gawain returned home."

"That's a neat story!" said Ronnie.

"Boy, and we're eating in a restaurant named after him," said Nancy. "That's neat. Sir Gawain must have been a great knight."

They all realized at once that Uncle Ron had said not a single word during dinner. Four pairs of eyes looked at him. They saw a very unhappy expression on his face.

"Tony Palermo escaped," he said quietly. "He was in a room inside the castle. There was an agent outside the door. The door was locked. But he escaped. And nobody can figure out how he got away."

"That pretty well proves him guilty, doesn't it?" suggested C.J.'s father. "He's a smart guy. If he could prove his innocence he would have stayed around. I know that type of guy. He would have loved bringing suit against the government for false arrest."

"That argument makes sense," said

Ron Watson. "But that still doesn't explain how he got out of a locked room. And it doesn't explain why C.J. had so many 'accidents' today.

"Listen, C.J.," said his Uncle Ron. "Please tell me once again everything that happened when you chased that guy out of the restaurant."

"Sure," said C.J. He, too, wanted to figure out just why he had become such a target. He told his uncle everything, every little detail. "The door swung open right out of the mirrored wall. By the time I got outside the guy had run off. The last time I saw him he was pushing that door open. So I guess he had a head start on me," finished C.J.

"You match up exactly with your first story," said Uncle Ron. "There are no new clues there. But you must have seen something. Otherwise they would not be after you."

"Any more counterfeit bills turn up?" asked C.J.

"Many, many hundreds of dollars have been turned in today," said Uncle Ron. "That means thousands more went home with visitors who made change in the shops and booths today."

"Does that mean that park employees are involved?" C.J. asked.

"That's the logical conclusion," said his uncle. "But we haven't been able to find any source for the money. Nor have we found any pattern in the discovery of bad bills. This is really a messy situation."

"How about if we go off to the ghost house," said C.J.'s dad.

"We've got a bulletin out on Tony Palermo," whispered Uncle Ron to C.J.'s dad. "We've got to keep an eye on C.J. I think Palermo is after him. That's the only explanation that makes sense."

C.J. saw that Nancy and Ronnie were doing some whispering of their own.

"Dad sure is keeping a lot of secrets today," hissed Ronnie.

"And I think counterfeiting is more than just his hobby," hissed back Nancy. "Just what does our father do for a living, anyway?"

"Maybe C.J. knows," whispered Ronnie. They both looked at their cousin. C.J. just shrugged his shoulders and threw up his hands.

"We're off for 'Merlin's Mysterious Mansion'," said C.J.'s father. "Our timing is just right. The sun has gone down. It's becoming dark and plenty spooky outside."

The line winding into the mansion was very long. They had nearly fifteen minutes to wait.

"Uncle Ron, how are counterfeit bills made?" asked C.J. "What steps does a counterfeiter have to go through?"

"A counterfeiter mainly needs the right paper and the right printing press," said Uncle Ron. "The perfect paper is made by Crane and Co., of Dalton, Massachusetts. But that paper is sold only to the government. Crane has not lost or had stolen one sheet of paper in the 100 years it's made paper for Uncle Sam.

"So a counterfeiter might buy paper very much like the real thing," continued Uncle Ron. "Then the faker might press blue and red lines into the paper.

"The printing presses are easier to come by. Many modern presses can print well enough to make money. The plates

53

are harder to make. They have to be engraved perfectly. A powerful acid is used to burn the images into the plates. Then a chemical is used to stop the burning at just the right time. If the stopper isn't used properly the plates are ruined.

"Counterfeit bills are tough to make," finished Uncle Ron. "Whoever is spreading them around here is a real pro."

"Uncle Ron, is the acid used on the plates the same as the acid used on the wax figures in 'The Sheriff's Jailhouse of Horrors'?" asked C.J.

"I don't know," said his uncle. "Why, do you think that might be important? What's the connection?"

"I don't know, either," answered C.J. "I feel like there is a connection here. But I can't quite put my finger on it."

A man dressed in the costume of an ancient warlock greeted the Watsons at the door to the mansion. He wore long robes with yellow moons and stars shining brightly. Atop his head perched a wizard's cone that ended in a sharp point.

"Greetings, hardy ones!" bellowed the warlock. "I am Modred, nephew of the

54

accursed Arthur. Merlin is my master. Come, and I will show you through his house of mystery."

They entered a room filled with bubbling beakers and boiling brews. Bats fluttered around near the ceiling.

"This is the room of the alchemist," said Modred. "His task in life is to turn the base elements into precious metals. Today he attempted to turn simple lead into solid gold. He failed. And for his punishment. . . ."

Modred led the way into the next room. A realistic wax figure stood inside a rope-covered machine. Ropes were tied to his arms and his legs. He was being stretched all out of shape.

"This is the rack, boys and girls," hissed Modred. "Do not fail Merlin, or his fate will be yours!"

Modred left the room. The lights went out. The floor began to move. C.J. heard a wall slide open. The door slid shut behind their group. The floor stopped moving. The lights went back on.

A curtain swung open at one end of the room. There stood an old man with a beard that trailed down to the floor.

"Merlin!" shrieked someone in the room. The old man chuckled and stepped across the stage. He swung an arm to the right. A blinding light flashed. There suddenly, magically, appeared on stage tables full of equipment.

Silently, Merlin ran through a series of magic tricks. He pulled rabbits out of hats. He poured milk from a pitcher into a handkerchief without spilling a drop. He produced a bouquet of fresh flowers and then turned it into a handful of snakes. He found eggs in his hair, behind his ears, and inside his mouth. The audience applauded his every magical move.

"And now, ladies and gentlemen, for my final conjuring feat of the evening!" Merlin had finally spoken. The voice was rich and full and friendly, C.J. thought. "For this special event I need a youthful volunteer from the audience."

A number of hands went up. Merlin seemed to be looking the crowd over. Suddently he pointed his wand. "You there. You are my choice."

C.J. looked behind him. He wanted to

see Merlin's selection. Everybody behind him was looking at C.J. and smiling. C.J. looked back at Merlin.

"Yes, you, young man. Please step forward," said Merlin.

"No, C.J., don't do it," said an urgent voice from C.J.'s right. That was Uncle Ron. "This might be a trap."

But the audience got in the way. People pushed C.J. up toward the stage. C.J., heard Uncle Ron pushing through the crowd. But it was too late. C.J. was suddenly standing next to Merlin the magician.

"Do not worry, young man," said Merlin. "No harm will befall you. Remember, I taught King Arthur the proper use of his Excalibur. So there should be no problem with my next trick. I am going to lock this youth into my box of mystery. Then I shall run a dozen swords through the box. Magically, this young man will remain unharmed. I hope you all get the 'point' of this trick."

C.J. heard laughter from the audience. Oh, no, he thought, no more swords. C.J. found himself edging away from the magician. But Merlin caught him by the collar of his shirt.

"No backing out now," chuckled the magician. He guided C.J. into the multi-colored box. C.J. sat down on the little bench seat. Merlin pointed to C.J. for all the crowd to see. Then he slammed the door and clicked the lock.

C.J. heard a tape recorder click to life. He felt the shakes starting up again. What a perfect trap, he imagined.

"In five seconds your seat will drop out from beneath you," said Merlin's voice on the tape. C.J. had to strain to hear the soft voice. "You will slide down the chute and land in a pile of soft pillows. Please turn to your right and walk up the stairs. Push open the door. You will end up on the right side of the stage. Wait for your cue. And then walk in with a big smile on your face. Thanks. And away we go."

The seat dropped out and the floor opened up. C.J. hit the chute softly. He slid easily down the chute. He landed bottom first in the pile of pillows.

The room was dimly lit. Shiny foot-prints on the bricks of the flooring showed him the way out. C.J. turned to the right. But he wondered what he'd find to the left. Maybe there was a whole world underground at "King Arthur's Adventureland." He found the door. He pushed against the door. It didn't budge. C.J. turned around. He looked in the shadows. Was that a footstep he heard behind him? Were they coming for him now?

C.J. backed up. He bumped the door again. This time it swung right open. The opening caught him by surprise. C.J. stumbled. He fell backwards. Reflexes took over. He executed a reverse somersault and landed cleanly on his feet. He heard a thunder of applause from behind him.

"And there he is, safe and sound!" exclaimed Merlin. "Not a sword wound on him, is there?"

People in the audience slapped C.J. on the back as he returned to his family. All C.J. could do was smile.

Merlin disappeared in a puff of smoke. The lights dimmed again. Once more the floor moved through what had just before been a solid brick wall. The floor stopped.

60

C.J.'s heart was still pounding from his experience. The lights came on, but only dimly.

C.J. could see a row of slowly moving chairs. The chairs moved along a track. They disappeared through a wall at the far end of the room.

"Friends in magic," said a taped voice through a loudspeaker. "The last part of our journey begins now. Please be seated in one of our magic carpets. You will be treated to the most magical five minutes of your lives."

People mounted the moving chairs in ones and twos.

"Al, you go first with Nancy," said Uncle Ron. "C.J., you go next. Ronnie and I will be right behind you."

C.J. watched his father and cousin duck into a chair. He ducked into the next chair. He heard his uncle and cousin Ronnie land in the third chair.

C.J. passed through the first wall. The huge room was filled with hundreds of sights and sounds. Ghost images seemed to crawl up the walls and disappear into the ceilings. Chains rattled and bones creaked. This was a neat haunted house! Ghosts danced and fought and sang and screamed. Music blared from ghostly instruments. The spirits of famous people drank tea together. C.J. imagined he saw Ulysses S. Grant and Andrew Jackson playing a game of "old maid" on a dusty card table. This counterfeiting business was really getting to him!

C.J. saw his father and Nancy as the chairs turned one corner. He saw Uncle Ron and Ronnie at the next turn. The room ended and the chairs went into another dark passage. C.J. wondered what would be in the next room.

The chairs rounded a left-hand curve in the dark. C.J. heard Nancy giggle. Then he heard a clicking noise beneath him. He felt his chair veer off to the right. The chair rode smoothly. The dark ride continued. There were no noises except for the sounds of his chair against the metal track.

"Dad," he said softly. No reply. "Dad," he said a little louder. Still no reply. "Dad!" he shouted. "Uncle Ron!" he yelled. No one answered. The slow ride continued in the pitch darkness. C.J. felt tiny in the huge chair. He dug himself into a corner. He felt like he'd been riding for hours. There were no sounds. The only movement was forward, with a downward slant.

Suddenly the chair stopped dead in its track. C.J. heard footsteps. He couldn't see a thing. He held up his hand. He couldn't even see his hand! The footsteps came closer. What could he do? The footsteps sounded like claps of thunder.

C.J. jumped up. He swung out wildly. He felt a strong hand grab his shoulder. Another strong hand groped for his mouth. C.J. felt something wet pressed against his mouth and nose. The smell was terrible. He pushed at the hand. Whoever it was had great strength. C.J. couldn't budge against his attacker.

C.J. felt his arms grow weaker. The terrible smell grew worse. C.J. felt his legs fall out from under him. The chair's seat felt like a pile of feathers. C.J. suddenly didn't feel anything at all. He collapsed in a heap in the corner of the chair.

V

"Clackety-clack! Clackety-clack! Clackety-clack!"

C.J. heard the sound over and over again. At first the sound was dim. He could barely hear it. Then the sound grew louder and louder. C.J. wondered where the sound came from. Then he knew the answer. The sound was inside of his head. He had a whopper of a headache.

"Clackety-clack!"

Something was turning over and over again. Something was rolling, metal on metal. C.J. realized the "clackety-clack" in his head also came from someplace else. He could feel the "clackety-clack" in the brick against which his face rested.

And then C.J. woke up completely.

C.J. didn't open his eyes. He tried to roll up to a sitting position. He had to try several times before he pulled it off. He sat on his hands. His hands were tied

64

behind him. They were tied tightly with coarse rope. The rope was the kind used to tie up bales of newspapers. C.J. had felt the rope before. He had helped a friend of his deliver a newspaper route.

C.J. realized that his mind was not completely together yet. A drug had probably caused the confusion. He kept his eyes shut. The drug had knocked him out. The ground was rough on his hands. He wondered where he was. Slowly he opened his eyes.

"I'm in a dungeon!" he exclaimed softly. "I'm in a real dungeon!"

C.J. looked around the room. The walls were made of blocks three feet tall by five feet wide. The floor was hard-packed dirt with gravel mixed in. The gravel bit into his hands. He shimmied around so his hands were uncovered. But they remained tied behind him.

C.J. began to put it all together in his head. He had been in the magical mansion. His chair had been diverted to a side track. At the end of the line he had been drugged, put to sleep. And now here he was. But where was he?

"We're under the ground, kid," came a voice from across the room.

"Huh?"

"I'm over here in the corner," said the voice. "They got me too."

C.J. looked around the room. Finally he found the owner of a voice. The voice belonged to an older, well-dressed man. The man was also sitting up. His hands appeared to be tied behind his back. His legs were tied together, too.

"Who are you?" asked C.J.

"You may call me 'the Wizard'," said the man. "But my real name is. . . ."

"Tony Palermo!" guessed C.J. "I saw your arrest this morning. You passed a bad bill. I heard you're about the best counterfeiter in the whole world. But I thought you had escaped this afternoon."

"First of all, I'm now the second-best counterfeiter in the world," said Palermo. "The first-best made the bill that I passed today. The twenty was so good that even I could hardly tell it was fake."

"And secondly, I didn't escape this afternoon," added Palermo.

"What?"

"I was kidnapped," said Palermo. "These two guys came right through the floor of my cell. They caught me by surprise. They drugged me and carried me off. And here I am."

"Who do you think kidnapped you?" asked C.J.

"Probably the real counterfeiters," said Palermo. "I'll bet they figured a pro like me could figure out their system. They probably thought I'd help the T-Men so I could get off the hook. I probably surprised them by being here. They didn't expect the best faker alive to show up."

"Did you get a chance to get a good look at the fake twenty you were caught with?" asked C.J.

"I got a decent look," said Palermo. "Why?"

"Could you tell me what printing process was used to make it?"

"The bill was engraved and run through a rotary press, an old one," said Palermo. "The plates were probably hand-drawn. Then they were etched. Blood was used to stop the acid etch. The ink wasn't the best. The paper was near perfect. The

68

paper was just a little too thick, probably a sandwich. But it felt like the real thing. The bills were aged with coffee or tea. And then they were mixed in with the real stuff in the park."

"You sure know a lot about counterfeiting!" said C.J. "What's this 'blood' that you mentioned?"

"Oh, that's the chemical that stops the acid from biting into the metal of the plates," said Palermo. "You sure have a lot of questions, pal. You're not with them, are you?"

"No, I think they picked me up for the same reason they got you," said C.J. "I guess they think I know something that can help the Secret Service. I chased one of the runners this afternoon."

"Well, you'd better be careful, kid," said Palermo. "If they plan on hanging around this park for very long, then they sure don't want us around. They might take us on a little trip."

"But if this is a one-day operation," added Palermo, "then they'll clear out and let us sit until the cops get in to rescue us. I guess we'll wait and see."

"You can wait if you want to," said C.J. "But, I'm getting out of this stupid dungeon."

"What are you going to do, cut yourself out?" asked Palermo with a laugh.

"That's exactly what I intend to do," said C.J.

C.J. dug his fingers into the pocket on the left side of the seat of his jeans. He grasped his tiny Excalibur and pulled it out. The knife clattered to the floor. C.J. managed to pull the knife from its scabbard. He pushed the handle of the knife into the hard dirt. He braced the hilt against the wall. Then he carefully slid the rope against the blade. He felt the rope give a little. Then the blade cut through one strand. Soon it cut through all of the ropes.

C.J. stood up and rubbed his wrists. The ropes had burned his skin a little. He slid Excalibur back into its scabbard. The knife dropped back into his pocket. He was ready to run.

"Hey kid, what about me?" screamed Tony Palermo.

"If you answer one question for me, I'll

70

cut you loose," said C.J. "But you have to promise to hang around the park until this is cleared up. That way your innocence can be proven."

"You got it, pal. What's the question?"

"Next to you, who was the best counterfeiter ever?" asked C.J.

"That's easy," said Palermo. "Emmanuel Ninger was the best. He operated in the late nineteenth century. He hand-drew all of his stuff. The T-Men got him, though, and he went to jail. He disappeared after he got out. Nobody knows what happened to him."

"I think I know what happened to him," said C.J. "Thanks, Mr. Palermo. You've given me all of the information I need." C.J. turned and opened the dungeon door and started toward the tunnel marked "Exit."

"Wait a minute, buddy!" shouted Palermo. "We had a deal. Cut me loose."

"Sorry about that," said C.J. He put Excalibur to work once more. Soon Palermo was free.

"What's your name, pal?" asked Palermo.

"You can call me Dr. Watson," laughed C.J. "That's short for C.J. Watson."

"See you around, C.J.," said Palermo. "And don't worry. I won't leave the park. A deal's a deal. Anyway, I want to see this thing solved."

"Good-bye, 'Wizard'," said C.J.

C.J. started back down the "Exit" tunnel. He heard Palermo trying a tunnel in the opposite direction. C.J. walked for a long time down the tunnel. There was very dim light and nearly no sound. The "clackety-clack" had come from the other direction. What was that sound, C.J. wondered? Why did Palermo head in that direction? Was it because the sound was familiar to him?

Finally there was a fork in the tunnel. The left hand fork was labeled "The Dragon's Cave." The right hand fork was labeled "Merlin's Mysterious Mansion."

"I've already been in the mansion," said C.J. "So I guess I'll visit the cave."

C.J. noticed the tunnel getting wider and wider as he neared the cave. He began running into park workers and passing offices and meeting rooms. He saw open-sided elevators and thin stair-cases. They all pointed up. He saw work-ers punching in and out of work. He saw restaurants and lounges and doors marked "break room." He realized he had dis-covered a city beneath the city of Came-lot. He was seeing the amusement park from underground. He was inside the guts of the machine.

C.J. continued to walk toward "The Dragon's Cave." He passed another "break room." The door was slightly ajar. He heard a familiar high-pitched voice. C.J. peeked into the room. Inside sat Mickey Dunn, the scop. With him was Sir Percival, his helmet perched on the table next to him.

"Well, I don't believe it!" bellowed Sir Percival with a roaring laugh. He ran a hand through his long red beard. "There's the bright young man I saw several times this day. What brings you down here, laddie?"

C.J. stood frozen to the spot. What could he do? "I'm just looking around, sir," said C.J. "I don't mean any harm."

"Perhaps you'd best run along, son,"

said Percival. "The security guards here run a pretty tight ship. They might not like your being here."

C.J. ducked out of the doorway. He walked quickly toward "The Dragon's Cave." Funny, he thought, Mickey Dunn hadn't said a word to him. C.J. passed a large pile of barrels marked "Dragon's Blood." It figures that "The Dragon's Cave" would need "Dragon's Blood," thought C.J. But why? "Dragon's Blood" had nothing to do with the blood of dragons. "Dragon's Blood" was used in the production of wax dummies. It was used on the bottom of the logs in the log flume. There were barrels of it in the print shop. So it was used in printing somehow.

"Printing!" exclaimed C.J. "'Dragon's Blood' is used in printing. That means it might be used in counterfeiting. Tony Palermo said 'blood' was used to stop the acid engraving the plates. 'Dragon's Blood' was used to stop the acid etching the wax figures. I'll bet they're the same thing. The counterfeiters are using 'Dragon's Blood'! And it's all over the

74

place in this park!"

C.J. realized he had been speaking aloud. His blood pulsed with excitement. He picked up speed. He had to get out of the underground city. He had to check the stockpiles of "Dragon's Blood." That was the key to this case!

C.J. followed the tunnel though it became thinner and seemed to be going slightly downhill. The lighting was good. At the end of the tunnel he could see someone running. He saw he was the runner. There was a mirror at the other end. He could see a staircase at the top of the mirror.

Then C.J. heard the sounds behind him. There was a rumble, a bounce like wood against stone. There was a slight sloshing sound.

The sound grew louder. Something was rolling through the tunnel! C.J. ran harder, pumping his arms and legs mightily. The staircase seemed a mile away. But it drew closer with every painful step. The crashing seemed right on his heels. He pushed harder and harder. The noise was right on top of him. He felt something huge looming over his shoulder. The tunnel was too thin for him to step aside. He had to make it to the staircase.

Fifty feet to go. C.J. felt something brush the back of his foot. That gave him the strength to push on. Twenty feet. The mirror reflected a blur. He couldn't see through the sweat in his eyes. Ten feet. He could make out his rushing form and a giant shadow chasing him. Five feet. The roar in his ears was deafening.

He jumped for the staircase. He grabbed the iron railing with shaking hands. He swung his feet out of the way. Just in time! The rolling attacker brushed against the bottom of his legs. There was an incredible explosion when the mirror shattered. Glass and liquid showered all over C.J. He hung onto the railing with all his might.

C.J. let himself drop to the ground. He made sure he landed on his feet. There was glass and nasty-smelling chemical all over the place. There were chunks of wood and a number of iron hoops and lots of nails.

This was no accident. C.J. had been chased down the tunnel by a barrel. Someone had pushed it after him. Someone had meant for C.J. to have a fatal accident. Someone was very scared of what C.J. knew.

But all C.J. could think about was the mirror. He had taken one good look into the mirror before the explosion. Mirrors reversed everything, including printed letters. But C.J. could still read the writing on the barrel. He had been run down by a barrel of "Dragon's Blood."

Mirrors reversed everything, C.J. repeated to himself. Then, with arms and legs trembling, he climbed the iron staircase into "The Dragon's Cave."

VI

C.J. entered "The Dragon's Cave" during a break between shows. He stepped into the main chamber. He closed the door behind him. The door sealed with a slight "click." He looked back. He could not find the door. The wall was solid rock.

C.J. walked over to the huge dragon in the center of the gigantic room. The dragon's head was thirty feet off the ground. C.J. ran his hand across the legs of the beast. The skin felt like a lizard's skin. This was one well-made dragon.

He was about to walk behind the dragon. He wanted to find out if "Dragon's Blood" was used here, too. But the public address system crackled to life. He heard a voice that sounded a lot like Mr. Stephen Greene, the Secret Service agent.

"C. J. Watson. C.J. Watson," repeated the voice. "Your mother and father are waiting for you at the main gate. C.J. Watson, please report to the main gate."

C.J. felt the blood rush to his head. He suddenly felt a sick feeling in his gut. He had forgotten all about his parents. He had been too busy tracking down the counterfeiters and escaping from their traps. His parents must be worried sick, he realized.

The P.A. system came to life once more. This time the voice belonged to a woman.

" 'King Arthur's Adventureland' will close in one half hour," said the woman. "Thank you for joining us on our very first day of operation. We hope you will join us again in the future. Tram buses will leave for the parking lots until 9:30 p.m."

C.J. felt he was being pulled in two directions. He knew his parents were terribly upset at his disappearance. He also knew that he could wrap this mystery up in the half hour he had left.

The dragon came to life. Steam erupted from its nostrils. A small flame exploded from its mouth. The dragon took a step

79

toward C.J. The flame grew larger.

C.J. stepped back from the creature. The creature took another step toward him. C.J. kept backing away until he hit solid rock. He was trapped between a rock and a fire-breathing dragon!

Suddenly the wall dropped back away from him. C.J. tumbled over. He came to rest against a metal column. He looked up. The metal column was the leg of a suit of armor. A knight towered above him.

"Well, what have we here?" laughed the knight. "I guess the young man wanted a sneak preview of the final show of the evening."

C.J. heard laughter. He looked behind the knight. A huge group of fair-goers were following the knight into the huge chamber. The dragon had only been warming up for the show!

C.J. didn't wait for the laughter to die out. He scrambled to his feet. He ran through the crowd and out the front door of the attraction. His mind had been made up. He had to solve the mystery. His parents would understand, he hoped.

C.J. walked quickly. He didn't run. He wanted to avoid attention. The security guards might be looking for him. He headed straight for "The Castle at Camelot."

C.J. ducked into the tent featuring "Ye Olde Castle Shops." He ran past the armorer's stall. Big John Curtis wasn't there. Another man pounded metal with a giant hammer. C.J. stood at the entrance to the print shop. A young man worked at the presses. He peeled layer upon layer of free ride coupons from the press. The press turned over and over with a "clackety-clack, clackety-clack, clackety-clack."

The young man spotted C.J. "Yes, young man, what may I do for you this evening?" said the printer.

"Is Mr. Ninger in?" said C.J.

"No, he's finished for the day," said the young printer.

"Do you use much of that 'Dragon's Blood' in here" asked C.J.

"Not really," said the printer. "Most of our work is done with photographic negatives. Those barrels are basically for show. They use a lot of the stuff at the log flume and wax museum, though.

"Do you use that Crane & Co. paper in making these coupons?" asked C.J.

"We sure do," said the printer proudly. "I'll let you in on a secret. Our coupons are exactly the same size as real paper money and the paper is almost exactly like real paper money. The only difference is the lack of red and blue lines. All of that is because we buy from the same company as the government."

"Is there an underground staircase that leads into the print shop?" asked C.J.

"Boy, you sure know your stuff," said the printer. "Yes, the whole castle is hooked up to the underground business area.

"You know," said the printer, "I was asked these same questions by this woman about half an hour ago. She really wanted to know all about 'Dragon's Blood'. She ran right off to the wax museum. Is that where you're going, too?"

"I believe it is," said C.J. "thanks for your help."

The printer waved to C.J. Then he clicked the presses back on. "Clackety-clack, clackety-clack, clackety-clack" went the rolling printing presses.

"Fifteen minutes to closing," repeated the woman's voice. "C.J. Watson, please report to the main gate. Your mother and father are waiting there for you. Fifteen minutes to closing."

C.J. ran down the path leading to "Nottingham Forest." He knew the answers now. He had to get into "The Sheriff's Jailhouse of Horrors" and "Little John's Magic Mirrors." He had it all figured out. He just had to prove it.

C.J. slowed down as he neared the wax museum jailhouse. There were very few people around. The park would be closing soon. C.J. knew he had to hurry. He rounded the last bend in the path before the wax house . . .

. . . when he was lifted off the ground from behind. A strong hand slapped over his mouth. C.J. struggled. A tall man held him off the gound. There was nothing C.J. could do. He was trapped, again. C.J. could see he was being carried to a fence. The fence stood near the entrance to the jailhouse. His kidnapper lifted C.J. high into the air. Then the man set C.J. down very gently on the other side of the fence.

C.J. was about to shout out for help when he heard a "Hush, C.J." from the dark nearby. The voice sounded familiar. His eyes adjusted to the dim light.

"Uncle Ron, Aunt Annie!" whispered C.J. excitedly. "I'm so glad to see you!"

"Your parents are worried sick about you," said Uncle Ron. "But I'm glad to see you here. You might be able to put your secret knowledge to use here."

"What secret knowledge?" asked Aunt Annie. C.J. noticed that his aunt carried a pistol in her hand. "Yes, C.J. Me, too," she chuckled. "Ron, what secret is this?"

"The counterfeiters have been after C.J. all day long," explained Uncle Ron. "Apparently C.J. saw something important when he chased their runner. Any ideas yet, C.J.?"

C.J. explained to his aunt and uncle about the "Dragon's Blood" connection. "That's the angle I've been working on all day," said his aunt. "We checked the park's records closely. A lot more 'Dragon's Blood' was used in the wax museum than could be accounted for."

"You knew that earlier today, Uncle Ron," said C.J. "Remember, you gave me a dirty look when I mentioned counterfeiting inside the jailhouse."

"We've searched the jailhouse since then, C.J.," said Uncle Ron. "But we came up empty-handed. There's nothing resembling a printing press in the whole place."

"I know where it is," said C.J. "And I think I know how we can get there."

"Show us the way, C.J.," said Aunt Annie, Secret Service agent. She barked orders to other agents to keep watch on the entrance to the jailhouse. "I outrank your uncle," she said with a chuckle.

C.J. led his aunt and uncle around back of "Little John's Magic Mirrors." He pointed to the "Exit" door.

"I came out there," said C.J. "The runner had disappeared by the time I got out here. But I wasn't that far behind him. I don't think he ever left the building."

C.J. trotted around to the main entrance to the house of mirrors. A tired-looking man stood at the ticket booth. "Sorry, we're closed," said the man "Come back tomorrow."

Uncle Ron and Aunt Annie flashed their badges and showed their pistols. "I guess we just reopened," said the ticket-taker with a hard gulp. He pushed a button, and the main door swung open.

"You wait here," Uncle Ron said to the man. "We'll want to talk to you when we're finished inside. Also, shut off all of the special effects. We're visiting on business, not pleasure." The man hit a number of buttons. Uncle Ron signaled into the darkness. A female agent stepped up next to the ticket-taker. He wasn't going anywhere. She would make sure of that.

The three Watsons raced through "Little John's Magic Mirrors." C.J. led the way past the trick mirrors, through the maze, and into that final room. The place seemed a lot less scary this time. The trio stopped in the middle of the room. They could hear a faint "clackety-clack" coming from nearby.

"This is the place," announced C.J. He pointed to the mirror with the "Exit" sign above it. "That's where I went out. And that's where I thought the runner went out."

C.J. walked over to the "Exit" mirror. "A person leaving through this door would be reflected in the mirror. Someone standing in the middle of the room would see the real back of the person **and** the reflected front of the person.

"I saw only the back of the runner," said C.J. "That means he wasn't going through this door. What it means is this: the runner was pushing through a mirror on the **exact** opposite side of the room. So his back was reflected in the "Exit" mirror. And that's what I saw when he escaped."

"That explains why they were after you all day today said Uncle Ron. "It looks like you're about to lead us into the den of the counterfeiters."

"Good job of deduction, C.J.," said Aunt Annie. "Well, Ron, shall we wrap this thing up?"

Uncle Ron found the mirrored panel exactly opposite to the "Exit" mirror. He pushed gently on the right hand side. The mirror swung inward slightly. "Clackety-clack, clackety-clack, clackety-clack" came loudly through the door.

Aunt Annie and Uncle Ron swept through the doorway. C.J. followed closely behind. They poured down the staircase, guns at the ready.

"Clackety-clack" roared from the fast-turning printing press. The noise drowned out the approach of the Watsons. Aunt Annie and C.J. ducked behind barrels marked "Dragon's Blood." Uncle Ron stood in the center of the room. His legs were spread wide. His gun was at the ready.

"Freeze!" shouted Uncle Ron loudly.

The two men froze. The "clackety-clack" continued. Sheets of twenty dollar bills poured from the press. Manny Ninger and Mickey Dunn slowly turned to face Uncle Ron. Their hands started moving into the air. They were giving up without a fight.

Uncle Ron stabbed his finger at the

"Off" button on the press. The "clackety-clack" slowly died out. Manny Ninger, the printer, and Mickey Dunn, the dwarf scop, had looks of disbelief on their faces.

"The kid!" barked the dwarf. He pointed at C.J. C.J. and his aunt had emerged from their back-up positions.

"Get that hand up!" ordered Aunt Annie. Dunn's tiny arm shot back into the air.

Uncle Ron handcuffed the two men. Aunt Annie read them their rights. C.J. stood there and smiled.

"Uncle Ron and Aunt Annie," announced C.J. "I think you'll find out that Manny Ninger is grandson to Emmanual Ninger, the famous counterfeiter. Apparently the knowledge of faking was passed down through the family. He hand-drew the bills for the plates. He used 'Dragon's Blood' to stop the acid etching the plates. He used Crane & Co. paper much like that used for real bills.

"Mr. Ninger tipped himself off early," added C.J. "The free ride tickets he turned out were much too well done and looked way too much like real money. I think he was showing off his abilities. I think he was laughing at the Secret Service. But he's not laughing now."

"Real funny, kid," said Ninger.

"Mickey Dunn was the main runner for the counterfeiters," countinued C.J. "We almost caught him with a stack of bills earlier, when Ronnie ran into him. I wondered why Dunn was always near Sir Percival. I realized that Dunn was using Percival's mesh basket to store fake bills. Since the bills looked like the free ride tickets, it was a perfect hiding place. Especially since the knight could not see the basket because of his armor. Whenever they neared a drop-off point, Dunn simply reached in for some fakes and passed them on. Sir Percival is a nice man. He was being used."

"Don't believe a word of it!" shrieked Mickey Dunn to Aunt Annie and Uncle Ron. "He's making it all up. I didn't know this was a counterfeiting operation. I just work here.

"By the way," added C.J. "I think Mr. Dunn might also face charges of attempted murder. He rolled a barrel of 'Dragon's Blood' after me down in one of the tunnels. I think you'll find his fingerprints all over the barrel.

"It was that barrel that helped me put all of this together," said C.J. "I saw the words 'Dragon's Blood' reflected in the mirror at the end of the tunnel. That's when I figured out the secret of the mirrored room."

Uncle Ron pointed to a staircase at the far end of the printing room. "I think we'll find that the stairs lead into the wax museum," he said. "That's how the supplies came in and out.

Aunt Annie marched the two prisoners up the stairs. They emerged through the floor of the wax museum. They were in a room with wax figures of the most famous criminals of all time.

"I don't think you guys will ever be honored in this place," said C.J. "Uncle Ron, I think you'll discover that they used these tunnels to kidnap Tony Palermo eariler. He didn't escape. These guys had him. Palermo is innocent this time."

92

"Very interesting," said Uncle Ron. "No wonder he turned himself in to us about an hour ago."

"He kept his word to me, then!" exclaimed C.J.

They went out the main door of "The Sheriff's Jailhouse of Horrors." They were greeted by a large group of Secret Service agents. Some agents went back down the tunnel to gather up the equipment. Two brawny men took the prisoners away.

"Mr. Greene," said Uncle Ron. Stephen Greene stepped out of the group. "I believe you can release Mr. Palermo. I have a lot of evidence showing he's innocent. In fact, you might even apologize to him for the inconvenience."

C.J. saw that many park employees had gathered to watch the arrest. Sir Percival was there. So was Big John Curtis.

"Uncle Ron," said C.J. "One more arrest has to be made."

"Who?" asked Uncle Ron. C.J. whispered into his uncle's ear. "Attempted murder, counterfeiting, and kidnapping!" hissed back Uncle Ron. "How?"

C.J. looked to where Sir Percival and Big John Curtis stood talking. "Watch," said C.J. to his uncle. "Sir Percival, who fitted you with your armor this morning? Who loaded your basket with free ride coupons?"

"Why, laddie, it was Big John here," said the knight. Sir Percival started turning toward the big armorer. Big John pushed hard on Percival's armor. The big knight toppled over with a crash. Curtis ran away.

"After him!" shouted Aunt Annie. "And now, young man, you'd best explain just why we're arresting this man. Uncle Ron told me that Curtis helped arrest Tony Palermo this morning."

"Of course he helped," said C.J. "That took pressure off his boss, Ninger. It also showed Curtis where Palermo was being held. He returned later through a door in the floor and kidnapped Palermo.

"Since he helped Sir Percival in and out of his armor he could easily load and unload bills from the mesh basket," added C.J. "That was a perfect set-up.

"But you also accused him of attempted murder," said Uncle Ron. "Explain."

"I believe he shot at me with an arrow on the pony rides," said C.J. "All of the arrows are made here. What better place to make them than in the armorer's tent. I also saw a huge form in the bushes before the attack. Big John is about the largest form in this whole place."

"That makes sense," said Uncle Ron. "Here they come now. He sure didn't give up without a fight." Big John was handcuffed. Six agents had hold of him. Several of the agents had bruises and torn clothing. Big John had been quite a tough arrest.

C.J. felt a tap on his shoulder. He looked around. Tony Palermo stood there, his hand outstretched.

"Good job, Dr. Watson," said Palermo. "We both kept our ends of the bargain. Thanks."

"You're welcome, 'Wizard'," said C.J. with a smile. They shook hands. "The Wizard" melted into the darkness.

"I guess that about closes the case," said C.J.

"Not quite," said Uncle Ron. "You

have to answer to your folks for disappearing. They're not going to treat this very lightly."

"Here they come now," said Aunt Annie.

"Ulp," said C.J.

C.J. tolerated the hug from his mother and tried to pull away from his father. C.J. blushed brightly.

"Aw, c'mon," said C.J. "I'm all right."

"In fact," said Uncle Ron, "your C.J. is a hero. He helped the Secret Service break up a counterfeiting ring." Uncle Ron winked at his brother. "I understand that he did a super job."

The P.A. system crackled to life once again. "'King Arthur's Adventureland' is now closed for the day," said the woman's voice. "Knights, please return all free ride coupons to the main gate."

"I guess we're off for the main gate," said Uncle Ron. "Before the night is through we'll recover most of the bad bills.

"Thanks to C.J.," finished Uncle Ron.

"I'm hungry," said C.J. "Breaking up counterfeiting rings really builds up my appetite. I could really go for a big burger with lettuce and tomato and pickles and catsup and . . .

"Let's go home," said C.J.'s dad. "I guess we'll get a hamburger for the hero of the day—our own knight of the round table."

". . . mustard and onions and mayo and a thick slab of cheddar cheese. And a milk shake and french fries.

"And I want real cheese on my hamburger," said C.J. Watson. "None of that fake stuff for me!"